Mama Rocks, Papa Sings

AN APPLE SOUP BOOK

An Imprint of Alfred A. Knopf • New York

Mama Rocks, Papa Sings

by NANCY VAN LAAN
illustrated by
ROBERTA SMITH

 Published in the United States of America by Alfred A. Knopf, Inc., New York, and simultaneously in Canada by Random House of Canada Limited, Toronto.
Distributed by Random House, Inc., New York.

Library of Congress Cataloging-in-Publication Data
Van Laan, Nancy.
Mama rocks, Papa sings / by Nancy Van Laan ; illustrated by Roberta Smith.
p. cm.
"An Apple Soup Book"
Summary: A little Haitian girl describes how her parents' house fills up with babies as relatives drop off their children on their way to work.
ISBN 0-679-84016-8 (trade) ISBN 0-679-94016-2 (lib. bdg.)
[1. Stories in rhyme. 2. Babies—Fiction. 3. Haiti—Fiction. 4. Counting.] I. Smith, Roberta, ill. II. Title.
PZ8.3.V47Mam 1995 [E]—dc20 93-39225

Book design by Mina Greenstein
Manufactured in Singapore 10 9 8 7 6 5 4 3 2 1

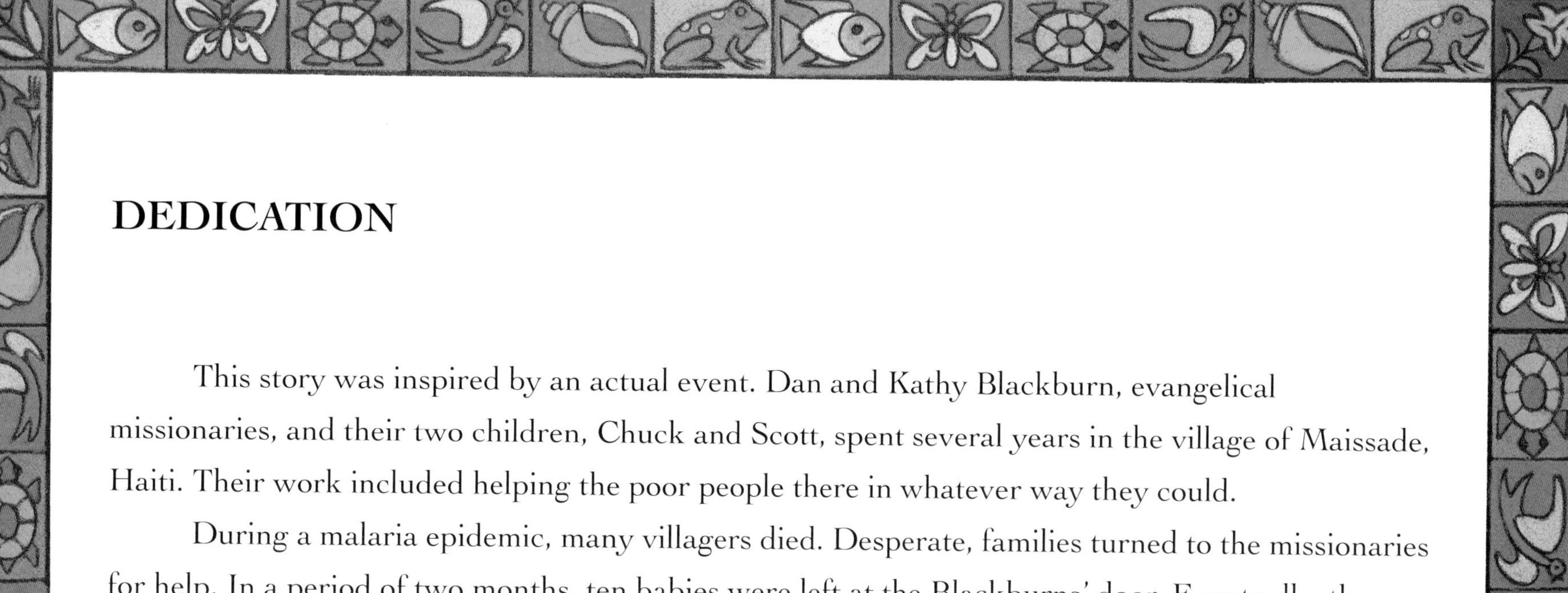

DEDICATION

This story was inspired by an actual event. Dan and Kathy Blackburn, evangelical missionaries, and their two children, Chuck and Scott, spent several years in the village of Maissade, Haiti. Their work included helping the poor people there in whatever way they could.

During a malaria epidemic, many villagers died. Desperate, families turned to the missionaries for help. In a period of two months, ten babies were left at the Blackburns' door. Eventually, these kind people adopted twenty-eight children, who, without parents, would probably have died.

When political upheaval rocked Haiti in 1986, the Blackburns and all their children fled the country. Finally, they made their way back to America and settled in their home state of Indiana.

Taking care of a family the size of a school class is a full-time job, so the Blackburns depend on the benevolence of others to feed and care for their children. This book is my gift to all of them: Dan and Kathy, Rosie, Mary, Yvonne, Rebecca, Jemima, Rachel, JoAnna, Cheryl, Lizzie, Marva, Abigail, Jim, Sam, Thomas, Bobbie, Steve, Jeremiah, Aaron, Ben, Matthew, Noah, Thaddeus, Gideon, Jake, Caleb, Mike, Mark, Andy, Chuck, and Scott. A portion of the earnings from this book will go directly to the Blackburns.

N.V. L.

GLOSSARY OF CREOLE WORDS

1	2	3	4	5
en	**de**	**twa**	**kat**	**cenk**
(en)	(day)	(twah)	(kat)	(sank)

6	7	8	9	10
sis	**sèt**	**yuit**	**nèf**	**dis**
(sees)	(set)	(yoo EET)	(neff)	(dees)

ba bay (bah BYE): good-bye
bamboché (bam boh SHAY): dance and have a good time
bon nuit (bohn nwee): good night
Bouki and **Ti Malice:** (BOO kee; tee mah LEES): Haitian folklore characters based on the tale of Anansi, the spider
chanté (shahn TAY): sing
dodo (DOH doh): rock, as a cradle

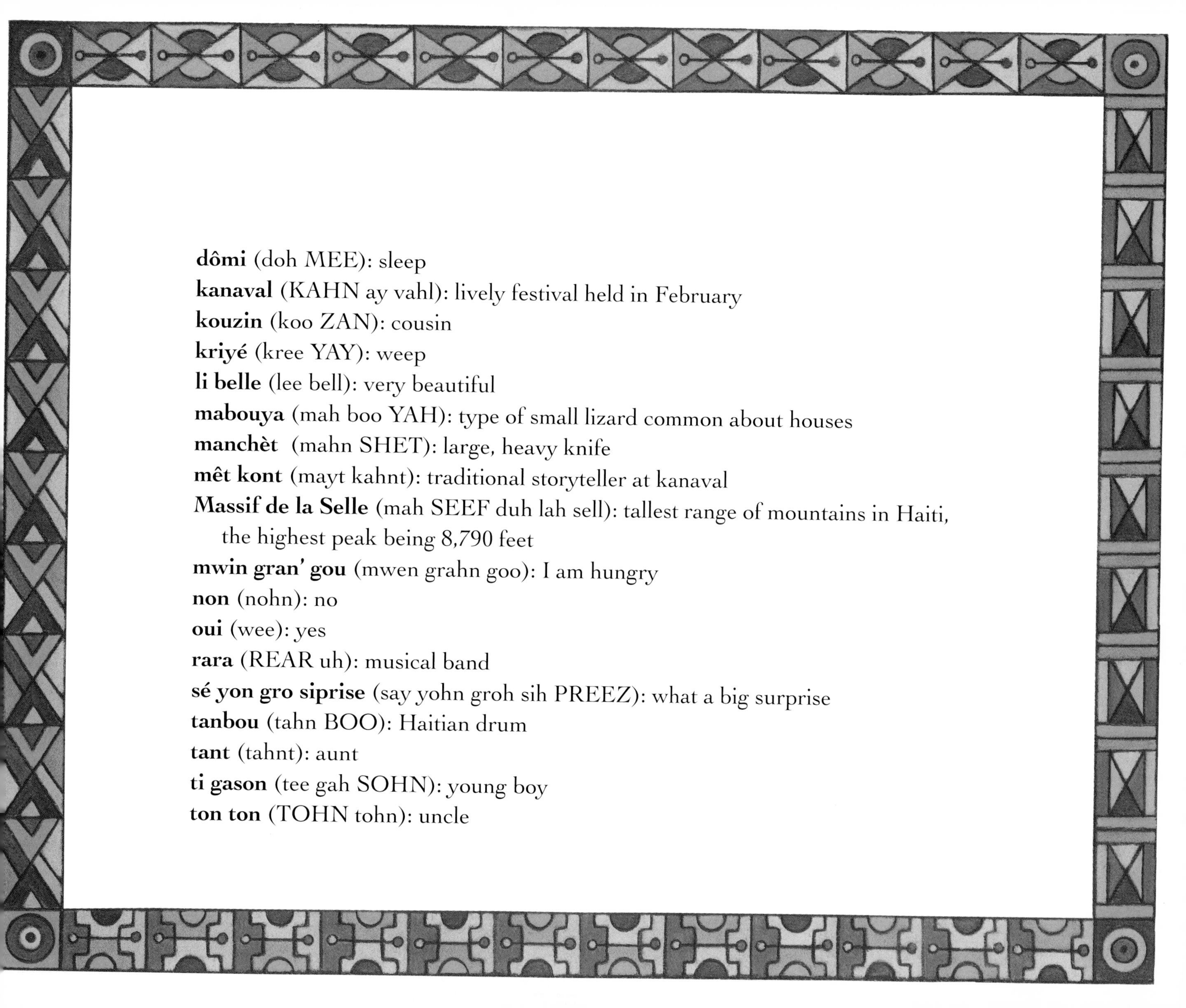

dômi (doh MEE): sleep
kanaval (KAHN ay vahl): lively festival held in February
kouzin (koo ZAN): cousin
kriyé (kree YAY): weep
li belle (lee bell): very beautiful
mabouya (mah boo YAH): type of small lizard common about houses
manchèt (mahn SHET): large, heavy knife
mêt kont (mayt kahnt): traditional storyteller at kanaval
Massif de la Selle (mah SEEF duh lah sell): tallest range of mountains in Haiti, the highest peak being 8,790 feet
mwin gran' gou (mwen grahn goo): I am hungry
non (nohn): no
oui (wee): yes
rara (REAR uh): musical band
sé yon gro siprise (say yohn groh sih PREEZ): what a big surprise
tanbou (tahn BOO): Haitian drum
tant (tahnt): aunt
ti gason (tee gah SOHN): young boy
ton ton (TOHN tohn): uncle

Mama and Papa live
in sunny Haiti, in hot Haiti,
all alone in Haiti.
Mama and Papa live
in poor Haiti, then—oh-oh!—

I come along and make three.

Wah! Wah! A baby on the floor.
Oui, oui! There is one more than before.
Woy-O! En-de-twa!
One-two-three!
Mama, Papa, me!

Put the baby in the cradle now
and wrap it all up.
Put the baby in the cradle now
and wrap it all up.
Mama rocks. ZI-ZAH ZI-ZAH
Baby weeps. WAH WAH WAH
Papa sings. SHU-LA SHU-LA
Baby sleeps. ZEH ZEH ZEH

Ton ton Eugène works
chopping sweet sugarcane.
He swings his sharp manchèt
back and forth—Zing! Zang!
While Ton ton chops, Tant Inez
weaves in a factory.
And guess what they do
with their little baby?

Oh-oh! A rat-tat on the door.
Oui! Oui! There is one more than before.
Woy-O! En-de-twa-kat!
One-two-three-four!
Mama, Papa, me, and kouzin Tyora!

Put the baby in the cradle now
and wrap it all up.
Put the baby in the cradle now
and wrap it all up.
Mama rocks. ZI-ZAH ZI-ZAH
Baby weeps. WAH WAH WAH
Papa sings. SHU-LA SHU-LA
Baby sleeps. ZEH ZEH ZEH

Around us live families
without enough to eat.
Friend Clive says, "Mwin gran' gou!"
He goes begging in the street.

No rice! Oh, no-no-no-no-NO!
No yam, no peas,
no corn to make the dough.

Oh-oh! A rat-tat on the door.
Oui! Oui! There is one more than before.
Woy-O! En-de-twa-kat-cenk!
One-two-three-four-five!
Mama, Papa, me, Tyora, and Clive!

Put the baby in the cradle now
and wrap it all up.
Put the baby in the cradle now
and wrap it all up.
Mama rocks. ZI-ZAH ZI-ZAH
Baby weeps. WAH WAH WAH
Papa sings. SHU-LA SHU-LA
Baby sleeps. ZEH ZEH ZEH

Papa paints a picture
while we play by the sea.
He paints Massif de la Selle;
he even paints me!

Next day he takes his art
to a big gallery;
ti gason trails him home—
sé yon gro siprise!

Oh-oh! A rat-tat on the door.
Oui! Oui! There is one more than before.
Woy-O! En-de-twa-kat-cenk-sis!
One-two-three-four-five-six!
Mama, Papa, me, Tyora, Clive, and Felix!

Put the baby in the cradle now
and wrap it all up.
Put the baby in the cradle now
and wrap it all up.
Mama rocks. ZI-ZAH ZI-ZAH
Baby weeps. WAH WAH WAH
Papa sings. SHU-LA SHU-LA
Baby sleeps. ZEH ZEH ZEH

Where we live on the mountain
trees grow close to the ground.
So, so many miles to go
by foot to any town.
When a naughty spider bites
Tant Julie on the hand,
no doctor's there to help her.
Ton ton does the best he can.

Oh-oh! A rat-tat on the door.
Oui! Oui! There is one more than before.
Woy-O! En-de-twa-kat-cenk-sis-sèt!
One-two-three-four-five-six-seven!
Mama, Papa, me, Tyora, Clive, Felix, and kouzin Devon!

Put the baby in the cradle now
and wrap it all up.
Put the baby in the cradle now
and wrap it all up.
Mama rocks. ZI-ZAH ZI-ZAH
Baby weeps. WAH WAH WAH
Papa sings. SHU-LA SHU-LA
Baby sleeps. ZEH ZEH ZEH

Mama stitches dresses,
very colorful, li belle!
She takes them in a basket
to the marketplace to sell.
When she drags home the basket,
what makes it so heavy?
We look inside and blink our eyes.
Do you know what we see?

Wah! Wah! A baby on the floor!
Oui! Oui! There is one more than before.
Woy-O! En-de-twa-kat-cenk-sis-sèt-yuit!
One-two-three-four-five-six-seven-eight!
Mama, Papa, me, Tyora, Clive, Felix, Devon, and Nate!

Put the baby in the cradle now
and wrap it all up.
Put the baby in the cradle now
and wrap it all up.
Mama rocks. ZI-ZAH ZI-ZAH
Baby weeps. WAH WAH WAH
Papa sings. SHU-LA SHU-LA
Baby sleeps. ZEH ZEH ZEH

Kanaval is here!
Time to sing and dance and eat!
We roast a goat and chicken—
what a fine, good treat!
While rara plays, we bamboché—
we let out such a roar!
Mabouya hides—and all the bugs,
they dance across the floor!

The mêt kont, he tells stories
all about Bouki.
That clumsy man fights Ti Malice
with great stupidity.
Everybody joins us—
what a wonderful party!
But when it's time to say ba bay,
not everybody leaves . . .

Oh-oh! A rat-tat on the door.
Oui! Oui! There are TWO more than before!
Woy-O! En-de-twa-kat-cenk-sis-sèt-
yuit-nèf-dis!
One-two-three-four-five-six-seven-
eight-nine-ten!
Mama, Papa, me, Tyora, Clive, Felix,
Devon, Nate, and twin kouzins,
Aveline and Benjamin!

Mama and Papa like
to hold the babies,
like to mind the babies,
take good care of babies.

Everybody's glad because
they love the babies.
But soon we are alone—
all the babies have gone home.

Again, it's Mama, Papa, ME!

Oh-oh! Is that a rat-tat on the door?
Non! Non! Papa plays tanbou!
Woy-O! En-de-twa!
One-two-three!
Mama, Papa, me!

Dodo, dodo, rock, rock.
Kriyé, kriyé, weep, weep.
Chanté, chanté, sing, sing.
Dômi, dômi, sleep, sleep.
Bon nuit, good night, bon nuit.

AFTERWORD

Haiti, the poorest and most densely populated country in the Western Hemisphere, is tiny—not much larger than the state of Vermont. It is located on the island of Hispaniola, where Christopher Columbus landed in 1492, thinking that he was in the Indies, near Japan or China.

The Taino Indians were its original inhabitants, and they named the island Hayti, which means "land of the mountains." Today, most Haitians are descendants of slaves imported by the French from Africa several hundred years ago. While French is the country's official language, Creole—a dialect of French that mixes African, Spanish, and English words, revealing the varied origins of Haiti's people—is more commonly spoken.

Most Haitians live in poverty, and many have moved to the United States in search of a better life. (In New York City, there are now nearly half a million Haitians, and Creole is the most common language—after English and Spanish—in the public schools.) But though they are poor, Haitians are rich in spirit. They celebrate their gift of life through vibrant music, dançe, art, and storytelling.

Some of the words in *Mama Rocks, Papa Sings* are Creole. The translators who kindly helped provide these words were Susan Woolfson, managing editor of the United Nations Association of the U.S.A., and Sauveur Dorcilien, a Haitian who now lives in New York. At the beginning of this book you will find out what each word means and a pronunciation key.